THIS BOOK BELONGS TO

~~Diddums~~   ~~Glenda~~

....

....

LADYBIRD BOOKS

UK | USA | Canada | Ireland | Australia | India | New Zealand | South Africa

Ladybird Books is part of the Penguin Random House group of companies
whose addresses can be found at global.penguinrandomhouse.com.

www.penguin.co.uk   www.puffin.co.uk   www.ladybird.co.uk

Penguin
Random House
UK

First published in Australia by Puffin Books 2022
This edition published in Great Britain by Ladybird Books Ltd 2023
002

Text and illustrations copyright © Ludo Studio Pty Ltd 2022

Printed in China

The authorized representative in the EEA is Penguin Random House Ireland,
Morrison Chambers, 32 Nassau Street, Dublin D02 YH68

A CIP catalogue record for this book is available from the British Library

ISBN: 978-0-241-55047-2

All correspondence to:
Ladybird Books, Penguin Random House Children's
One Embassy Gardens, 8 Viaduct Gardens, London SW11 7BW

MIX
Paper from
responsible sources
FSC® C018179
FSC
www.fsc.org

BLUEY

BABY RACE

Bluey, Bingo and Mum are at the playground. Bluey wants to know if she is better at the monkey bars than Bingo. "Well, you *are* two years older than her, Bluey," says Mum. "Am I better than Judo?" asks Bluey.

"Bluey," Mum says, "just run your own race."
"Huh? What does that mean?" Bluey asks.
"Come here,"
Mum says, smiling.
"Have I told you the story of when you took your first steps?"

"It all started when you were still a **baby** . . ."

"You learned to roll over really early," explains Mum.

"Were you proud of me for rolling over so soon?" asks Bluey.

"Yes," says Mum. "A little too proud. I think I may have turned into a bit of a show-off."

"But then one day at mothers' group . . ."

Judo sat up all by herself.

"But it was a race," says Bluey.
"A baby race!" shouts Bingo.

"I don't know what got into me," Mum admits. "But I was determined
I'd get you walking before Judo's mum . . . I mean, Judo."

THERE YOU GO . . .

STEADY . . .

BANDIT!

SHE'S SITTING!

But, by the time Bluey was sitting, Judo was crawling.

GOODNESS, I JUST CAN'T KEEP TRACK OF HER.

"Judo beat you again!" says Bingo.

"And just what did *you* do about this?" asks Bluey.
"I tried my best . . ." says Mum.

COME ON, BLUEY. CRAWL TO MAMA.
YOU CAN DO IT! YOU CAN DO IT!

"Did I do it?" asks Bluey. "Did I crawl?"
"Not exactly . . ." says Mum.

"Why was I *rolling*?" asks Bluey.
"I don't know, kid. You didn't
come with instructions."

"The doctor said there was nothing to worry about."

"We tried to show you how to crawl."

HOW GOOD IS
CRAWLING . . . ?

IT'S BETTER
THAN ROLLING.

"Did I do it?" asks Bluey.
"Did Bluey crawl?" asks Bingo.

"Nope," Mum says with a laugh.
"You were a bum shuffler."

"Meanwhile, Judo was pulling herself up on furniture, which is the step right before walking."

"We kept trying . . ." explains Mum.
"Did she crawl?" asks Bingo.
"Yes . . ." says Mum.

"Backwards!"

"None of it mattered, though . . ." says Mum.

"Judo had won the baby race."

"Were you upset with me because I lost the baby race?" Bluey asks. "No, sweetie," says Mum. "We were all learning to do things for the first time. I just felt like I was doing everything wrong."

"But, one day, Coco's mum
came over to see me," says Mum.
"We chatted for a while, and then
she showed me a photo."

"'Are these all your children?' I asked. 'I thought Coco was your first. Wow, you must have learned a thing or two.'
"'I have,' she said. 'And there's something you need to know . . .'"

"Are they happy tears,
Mum?" asks Bingo.
"Yeah, happy tears,
honey," says Mum.

"From then on, I decided to run my own race."

WOOHOO!
BLUEY WINS!

"So, did Bluey ever learn to walk?"
asks Bingo.
"Yes, honey. In the kitchen,"
says Mum.
"Why did I decide to walk in
the kitchen?" asks Bluey.
"I don't know, sweetie," says Mum.
Bingo thinks . . .

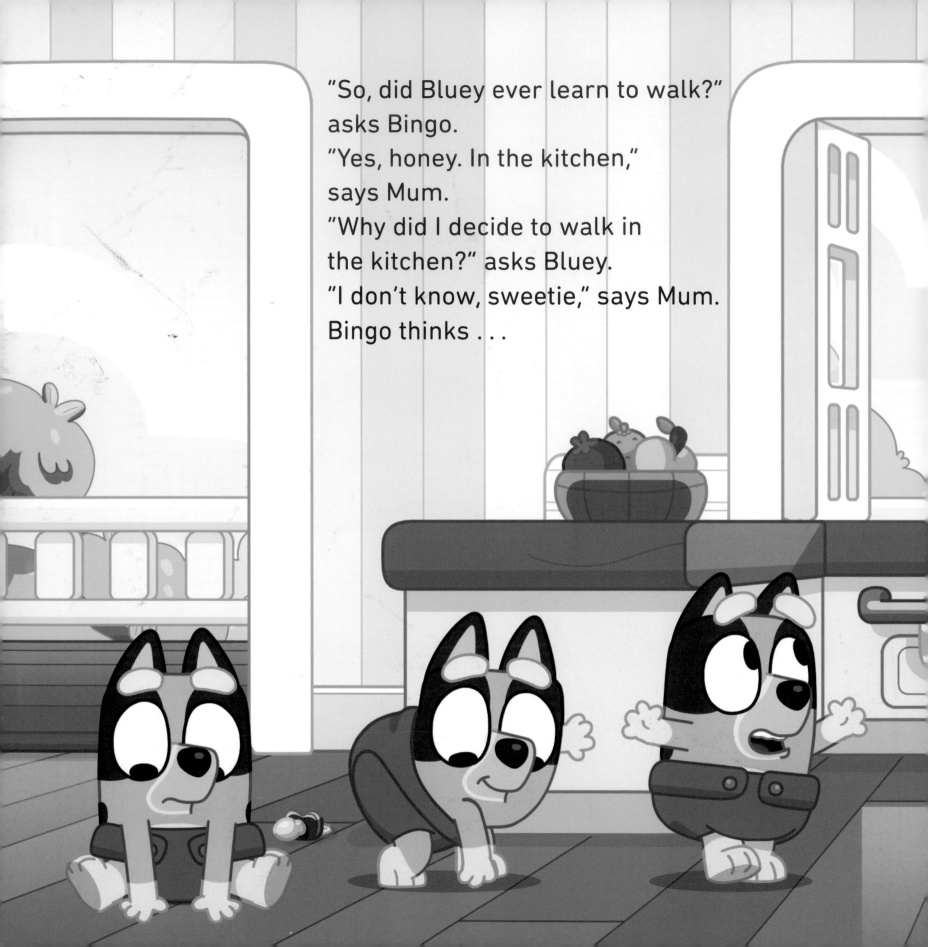